POKÉMON

DP BATTLE DIMENSION

Triple Trouble

BASED ON THE EPISODE "THE THIEF THAT KEEPS ON THIEVING"

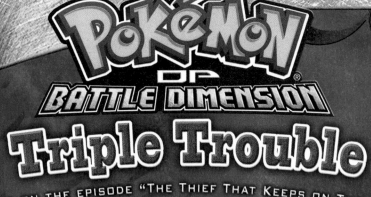

BY SIMCHA WHITEHILL

SCHOLASTIC INC.

New York   Toronto   London   Auckland   Sydney
Mexico City   New Delhi   Hong Kong   Buenos Aires

ISBN-10: 0-545-11210-9
ISBN-13: 978-0-545-11210-9

© 2009 Pokémon. © 1997–2009 Nintendo, Creatures, GAME FREAK, TV Tokyo, ShoPro, JR Kikaku.
Pokémon properties are trademarks of Nintendo. All rights reserved.

Published by Scholastic Inc.
SCHOLASTIC and associated logos are trademarks and/or registered trademarks of Scholastic Inc.

12 11 10 9 8 7 6 5 4 3 2 1   9 10 11 12/0

Designed by Cheung Tai and Henry Ng
Printed in the U.S.A.
First printing, May 2009

Ash, Dawn, Brock, and Pikachu were on their way to Pastoria City. Suddenly, a Pokémon landed right on Dawn's head!

Dawn took out her Pokédex. It was a Bug-and-Flying-type called Yanma.

Yanma flew away. Just then,
a boy ran up to the crew.
"Have you seen a Yanma?"
he asked.

Everyone decided to follow the flying Pokémon.

The boy brought out his Piplup. Together, they tried to catch Yanma.

But Yanma got away.
"We missed again. We will
get it next time," the boy said.

"I'm Tyler and this is Pippy," the boy continued.

"Nice to meet you!" Ash said.

Tyler had just started his Pokémon journey. He had followed Yanma for three days.

Dawn and Ash knew how hard it was to be a new Pokémon Trainer. They offered to help Tyler make his first Pokémon catch.

As they looked through
the woods, Staravia spotted
Yanma.
    Tyler and Pippy snapped
into action!

Tyler was about to catch
Yanma when he heard a splash.
"Oh no! It's Team Rocket!"
cried Ash.

Jessie, James, and Meowth
stole Yanma away from Tyler!
"We love it when the twerps
do all our work!" Jessie said.
Dawn's Piplup swam after
Team Rocket, but their Feebas
submarine was too fast!

Tyler was so upset, he started to cry.

But Ash told Tyler not to give up. Together, they would catch a Yanma!

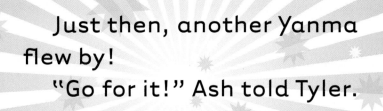

Just then, another Yanma
flew by!
"Go for it!" Ash told Tyler.

But Team Rocket had crept
up on them again! They wanted
another Yanma.

Ash, Tyler, Brock, and Dawn
were determined to stop them.

Ash called on Chimchar.
Jessie yanked out Yanma.
James chose Carnivine.
Even Meowth moved in.

All of a sudden, something started to happen to Jessie's Yanma.

"Whoa! It's starting to evolve!" Meowth yelled.

Yanmega's SonicBoom sent a very strong wind. *Whap!* Ash, Brock, Dawn, Tyler, Pikachu, Piplup, Pippy, and Chimchar ran for cover.

Luckily, the new Yanma escaped before Team Rocket could grab it.

But Jessie, James, and Meowth got away, too!

"Oh no! I messed up again,"
Tyler said sadly.
But Brock had a great idea
for the new Trainer.

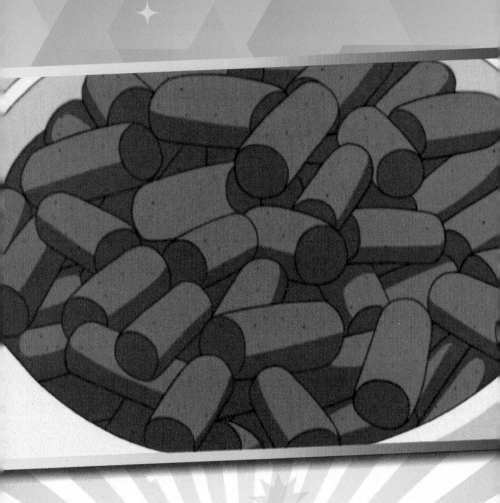

Brock made special Pokémon food with Yanma's favorite fruits. He placed it in a bowl by the river.

A Yanma flew right up to have a snack!

"Okay, Pippy, now's our chance!" Tyler cried.

Pippy knocked out Yanma with one Pound! *Pow!*

"Way to go, Pippy!" Tyler shouted.

But before Tyler could throw his Poké Ball, Team Rocket returned.

Ash broke out Buizel. "All right, use Aqua Jet!" he yelled.

Even Team Rocket's Yanmega was no match for the powerful Pokémon.

Zap! Pikachu blasted Team Rocket off with Thunderbolt!

Now it was up to Tyler and
Pippy to catch the new Yanma!
Pippy used BubbleBeam.
Yanma dodged it by flying
over the river.

Pippy dove into the water to chase Yanma.

"Wow! Look at Pippy go!" Dawn cheered.

Pippy brought Yanma back
to the shore.
But Tyler still could not
catch it in his Poké Ball.

"Give it one more try!" Ash said.

So Pippy gave Yanma another Peck.

Tyler tossed his Poké Ball.

This time it worked! Tyler and Pippy had caught their first Pokémon!

"Congratulations!" Brock said.

"I could not have done it without your help!" Tyler told his friends.

"That's what pals are for!" Ash said with a smile.

Now that he had caught
Yanma, Tyler was excited for
another adventure.

"Take care!" Dawn said.
She waved good-bye.

Ash gave Tyler one last
tip for his trip. "Find some
buddies to travel around with.
New places are fun, but old
friends are the best!"